ISBN 979-8989770106

Published by Hidden Hand Press

HIDDEN HAND PRESS

ISBN 979-8-9897701-0-6

Published by Hidden Hand Press
www.hiddenhandbooks.com

CHAOS:

Remnants of
Ruptured Reflections

by: Hamant Singh

CONTENTS:

Part I: HEAD

Part II: CHAOS

Part III: TAIL

Foreword
by
Shea Bilé

Past the tapestry enveiling the Great Womb, one ascends to become ashes—the dust of the divine, visible only when it is carried along by a twilit in-between. To descend below the sacred Kelipotic husks, one must extend their death, immolate and sublimate in the impossible shadow of a stubborn Sun—a Phoenix-cycle covered in its own ashes and unraveling eternally—the dying breath of Creation. This is what Singh does in this tome of Chaotic reflections.

Each poem here might also be read as a progressive invocation—a rite of sacred absurdity and a blasphemous widdershins ritual that bathes the Celebrant in the very light that will drown them, bringing their bodies past a transcendent veil of shadow, freeing them in their final successive breaths. In this way, Chaos is a book of "ruptured reflections"; further still, these poems are a tome dedicated to a fragile eternity, the nameless gods of a "Primordial Precedent."

Herein, Singh has painted with an ink made of fleeting dreams and scribed with the blood of something impossibly pure. A sage canonizing an ancient muse, then in the same moment, sacrificing her on the altar of his own ecstatic undoing. Here, Singh instructs us on the ways of falling in love for a final time.

What follows is a gateway to a terrible liminality, inescapably ecstatic, a Luciferic liberation of light, shadow, and something else entirely. Take this sage's hand and let him guide you past the path of screams, past the field of roses unraveling, and offer yourself on the altar of your own undoing. In your final breaths, your heart will beat for the first time, and you will see a world beyond beauty, a symphonic silence, a Chaos that cradles painful truths and makes gods of Man.

Shea Bilé
Lughnasadh, 2023
Los Angeles, California

Binaries or dichotomies are very simplistic ways of looking at concepts or issues in life. Dichotomies only exist when we consider things at a very fundamental level. Yet when we explore a grey area in between, we do not find a third static state. Instead, we are faced with unstable chaos. For instance, dusk is neither day nor night but is in a constant state of change and progression. It is not defined by either concept and does not exist in one pure form. Order *is* the demiurgic response to Chaos, which is the primordial precedent. Polarities or dualities were created to establish a fragile structure of order.

The poems in this text are intended to be read in pairs as it was written, with the end culminating in a chaotic middle. It was deliberately arranged this way to challenge conventional reading habits. However, it seems that the only genuine way to read it is in whichever manner the reader deems worthy. Another aspect of the poetry in the book is the chaos that breathes within each poem. Although any particular poem does lean towards one binary or the other, there is a constant and chaotic oscillation between both extremes. Chaos was deliberately sewn into the seemingly separated seams of the text.

The concept of this text may bring to mind William Blake's *Songs of Innocence and Experience*. Although Blake's poetry is legendary, this collection never intended to mirror his work. Just as my earlier work, *The Sibyl*, was a revisitation of Shelley's exploration of the Sublime, this text may be considered an advancement of Blake's writing. The text examines dualities and aims to eventually shatter them. The intention was to smash mirrors to create fractured bits of binaries; remnants of ruptured reflections, if you would.

Although this is a relatively short text, it is a pithy publication that is an extended hymn to Chaos itself. It is hoped that this collection will occupy a suitable position on your bookshelf.

Acknowledgements

I dedicate this collection to the hungry Abyss. Hail Azerate, Hail Chaos.

I would like to thank my family and friends for constant support of my writing. Also special thanks to the maestro, Izzard Padzil (MY) for the cover art to this text. To Arthur and Ryan DeHart of Naked Cat Publishing, thank you for the amazing amount of support. Both of you are fantastic as publishers and as people. Thank you to that unseen force that guides my hand and my writing. I don't know who or what you are but please keep working through me.

A very special mention goes out to Shea Bilé for writing the foreword to this text. Thank you, brother. It truly is an honour and I am humbled.

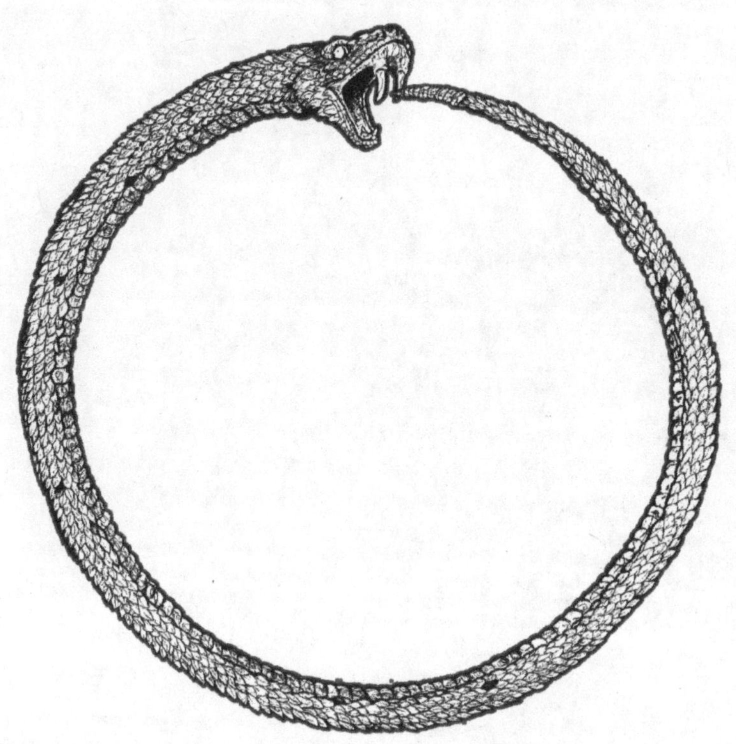

Part I:
HEAD

Sheep

Daytime bleats
To the beat
Of your shepherd's staff.
He calls and you heed –
Your need
To be meek.
The shepherd's keep.

How gentle and sweet
Your tunes
Ring into the sunshine!
Ambling
Through pastures
In a mindless meander
Of bounty.
O the rewards we reap
From herding sheep.

When the sun retires the shepherd,
There begins an unseeing.
An unbleating
Darkness –
The unforgiving veil
That is fuel
For ferocious wolves.
They devour
Ones that cower
And blood stains purity.

When a howl impales a bleat –
O the rewards we reap
From peering deep.

The Virgin

The white robe
In darkness,
I see with my eyes closed.
Sadness painted over
Your pale beauty.
The holier they paint you,
The hungrier I grow.

Longing to soil your white veil;
To taint your taint,
With each gentle tap
Of the tip of my tongue —
To stain that place
Where secrets lie.

Longing for that crimson rush;
Scarlet waves to fully flush
Your pallid cheeks.
Sinful fires that burn bright and
Hot on your breath.

Longing to watch you writhe,
As I carve obscenities on
The inside of your thigh.
Painting vulgarities in white
With a throbbing paintbrush,
While you wail
Like a banshee in the night.

I encounter you
Begging
On your knees –
In a sense,
Lost.
Pray for us sinners now,
And at the hour of our death.

Amen.

Roses

Shields that protect the core –
Time weathers away
Each layer.

Carefully arranged, to
Conceal the secret.
How did that infernal spiral,
The nefarious lie,
Rise above
Rows of thorns?

High and mighty,
It starts to fall.
Time weathers away
Each layer.
Riveted,
We watch
The demystification –
And take some steps toward the sacred.

And the last veil falls,
Exposing the guarded secret –
Naked,
Powerless.
We watch
Darkness at its core.

Our gaping mouths,
Our empty eyes,
The deafening silence
Reflects the brazen void –

Nothingness.

A Wave of Words

I stand
On your brink
As your waters
Wash my feet.

How would you know
What I dripped
Was for you
To be drunk?
To lick the salt
Off my words
And trust?
I would rather drown.

I greet you humbly,
Mighty onslaught!
Belittled as I am,
Beholding
Waves that form,
That lap the shore.
As your waters
Tempt my feet.

Drops of ocean
Scooped and drunk
In handfuls,
Leaving me thirsty for more!
Drinking more until I
Drown in madness!

Behold!
Gawking birds that fly above
But never submerge themselves.
For this is not their world.

Momentary stirs
That threaten foundations.
Scum that agitates,
Scuttling
On the floor below.

This is what I read.
But that is
Not what you meant.

The VVitch

Students of the planets
In perpetual retrograde.
Hollow apothecaries
Full of herbs and flowers,
Full of meaningless magic.
Where every day is Halloween
And everyone is a witch,
Mindlessly balancing
On the Rule of 3.

How did time
Stir that cauldron?
That turned
A hex into sex,
Potions into lotions,
Curses into purses.
O how sorcery has turned
To saucery.

What happened
To those they hung?
I still hear them
Carried on the wind.
I still hear them
Mumble, spit and cackle.
I still hear them
When the heavy branches creak –
The bloodstained earth
Rich with their eternal curses.

Where have all the vvitches gone?

Breath

To wet and warm
Your lips
As it passes through.
That you know
You are alive;
That you are not dead.
Yet, there is so much more to life
Than breath.

Our hungry, heaving chests,
Sweaty in the morning sun.
Our breaths that swirl
In that joke called love –
Where we are most alive,
Making us laugh until
You leave me
Breathless.

And we measure in breaths
With laughs and sighs.
That life
Is only
A wheezing moment
That blows in the wind.
Since the sum of all breaths
Culminate in one
Extended exhale.
Yet, there was so much more to life
Than death.

You are
A mere breath in life
And then no more.
You are
A mere sigh in a *phralaya*
And no more.

Part II:
CHAOS

The Circle

The meandering river
That found no end.
Profound ascent –
Only to find
His foot in his mouth.

Do I eat the skins
To learn?
Only to see my face reflected
In your infinite eyes of black.
Do I huff on your slough
To see
The evil face of K'uk'ulkan?
Or do I meditate on your moult
To understand
How Jörmungandr found his way
Around the world?

I leave my shell behind –
Red flesh
Exposed and tender.
I slither through
Every lie whispered,
As each whip settles
Into reptilian armour –
Dishonest scales.
I have become
The wise Old Man.

I now lie
Coiled and profound.
My breath is
Heavy and burdened
As I wait for
The tip to meet the teeth –

Only to find
My foot in my mouth.

Part III:
TAIL

Has He Ever?

Has He ever
Whispered in your ear
And made you tremble
And shake with fear?
A breath
That squeezes your heart
And forces
A cowardly drop
Down your face.

Has He ever
Passed you by –
A freezing
Zephyr of the future
That paralyzes your footsteps?
Unfamiliar mumblings
Of a familiar voice,
Muy familiar.
Tohu wa-Bohu beckoning
A return to the Otherside –
A previous one.

Has He ever
Held your shoulder,
Held your present
With warnings
Of the things to come?
How icy his grip is!
Devoid of affection,
Yet the void echoes
With his solemn promise.

Have you ever
Felt his frigid, rigid blade
Teasing the nape of your neck?
His murderous threat is law
Beyond time and space!
Chaos that lurks and haunts
Your shortened days.

Has He ever?
No
He must never;
And you can never!

The Warlock

Listen to the way
His silence blends
Into the graveyard gale.
The artist
That paints the stars
Black
And negates the night sky.
He that paints
The vengeful voices
That moan in the wind,
And swirl into
His malicious masterpiece.

Aeons of wisdom
Consciously condensed into
Potent poetic paintbrushes,
Dripping with blood magic.
Dry tools of old
Charged
With caked lips
Of those that cursed before.

Mumbling magic
Into Rotten ears
Of the dead,
The painting
Raises an army
Ravenous and rabid.

The single exhale,
The breath of death
That eats witches alive.

Describe The Scribe

Dreaded drought that dries up seas,
Tragic cloud of death, disease.
Drinking dry the seas of tears,
Pen that writes as chaos nears.

Wand of magic black as night,
Curses scribed by firelight,
Whispers, mumbles, hexes fly,
Spellbound, strangled till ye die!

Tomes of cold and darkness tell
Secrets, lies abound in hell.
Mystic knowledge whispered deep
In my ears and mars my sleep.

What is this that guides my hand?
Words and wit that do withstand
Time and taste of every creed.
Writing, writing till I bleed!

Blind compulsion fills the shelves,
Books that seem to write themselves!
Drink my tears and poison moans
Let my magic pierce your bones!

Tales of lust and wild disgust,
Myths unwrit you must distrust!
Write I may. Nay, must, I must!
Till my body turns to dust.

Thorns

What am I to do
With these
Fragments of life
That I clutch on to
With bleeding hands.

Rejections of beauty,
Discarded scraps
That grow ugly.
Grey teardrops –
Undesired souvenirs
That dull
By the hand of time.
I watch
Fingernails
Turn into food
For hungry scavenger ghosts.

They refuse to rot,
Hardened weapons
That protect
The crown –
Blackened sky
That makes stars shine bright.

I shall swallow these crumbs
And weave a string of spit,
For a new crown.
For there is much beauty
In the blood of a Messiah.

The Whore

Your red robe
Of darkness
I see with my eyes open.
How the abject strikes fear
In the feeble hearts of the blind.

I seek you out
At the mouth of
The hungry Abyss,
Great whore of Chaos!
I find you
Waiting for me
On the pathless path,
With your legs wide open.

Where you are the harlot,
To those who surrender.
Where you remain a virgin,
To those who are deaf to
Your name.

My hymns of adoration
Are soundless screams.
Mere echoes drowned
In the howling winds of
Your stormy silence.

I kneel before
The Great Whore,
Ready to take you in my mouth.
Drinking deeply
From the blessed effluvium,
That I may be worthy
To take an infinite sip of
The Great Yoni.

O euphoric ecstacy!
Face to face with
The immaculate!
I stumble and
Drown in
Your deep cup of whoredom!

Wolf

Form revered,
That men desire
To shapeshift into
Your savagery.
Vicious strikes
As the trained, pointed
Scythe of Death.

Your majesty,
Elegance enthroned!
To arrive as a feral beast
And transform
Into terror itself.
Starving Chaos
Weaving magically
Between the softest fur.

Chaos
That breathes
In your piercing stare;
The abyss
That beckons
In your hungry snarl.
That deafening silence
Before innocence is shredded
By bloodstained fang.

The dark is sacred in
Your prowl by moonlight;
The quiet is scarred from
Your howl at midnight.

Hamant Singh is a Singaporean writer who is inspired by the Sublime in horror, different cultures and the occult. *CHAOS: RRR* is his second release after *The Sibyl* in December 2022

After a poem was nominated for the 2022 Rhysling Award by the Science Fiction Poetry Association, *The Sibyl* was listed on the preliminary ballot for the 2023 Bram Stoker Awards (Superior Achievement in a Poetry Collection). In 2023, *The Sibyl* was also nominated for the 2023 Elgin Award. Hamant currently resides in the mountains of Chiapas, Mexico where he is currently working on an art/poetry collaboration with Irish artist, Shane Reilly.

His next release, NÁUSEA | CONFESIÓN is a collaboration with Mexican author, Pedro Tsamaxan. Hidden Hand Press will release this collection in 2024.